# How to Get a Gorilla Out of Your Bathtub

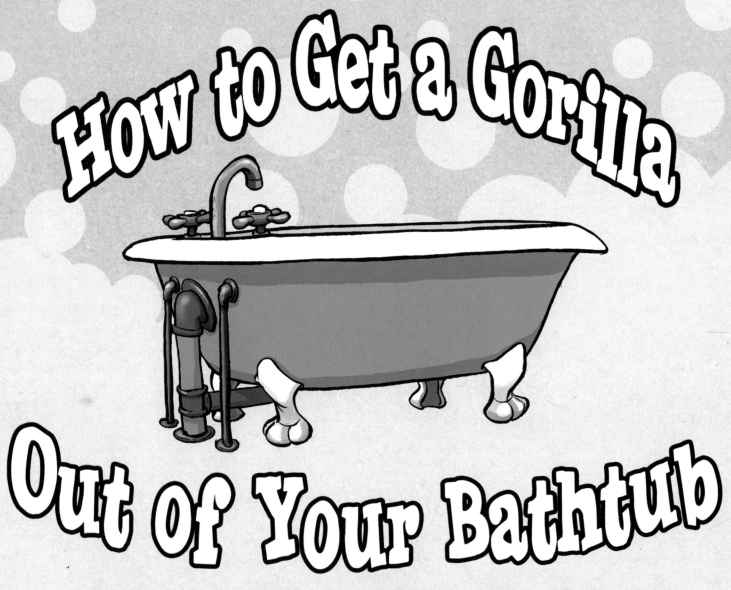

written by John Hall    illustrated by Stephen Gilpin

a Red Rocket Bookworks creation

published by

WHITE STONE BOOKS
LAKELAND, FLORIDA

How to Get a Gorilla Out of Your Bathtub
Copyright © 2006 Red Rocket Bookworks, Inc.
ISBN: 1-59379-070-8

A Red Rocket Bookworks creation,
Published by White Stone Books
P.O. Box 2835
Lakeland, Florida 33806

Typesetting by nbishopsdesigns

First Edition

09  08  07  06          10  9  8  7  6  5  4  3  2  1

To E.M.,
who would give the Gorilla lots of ideas for even more creative day trips.

To J.G.,
who would want to wrestle the Gorilla just to say he'd done it.

To D.B.,
who would become very best friends with the Gorilla
before the day was out.

To G.G.,
who would have the Gorilla all clean and tucked into bed,
reading him a story.

To J.J.,
who would just laugh and jump into the tub with the Gorilla.

J.H.

For Talulabel, because she always thinks she knows what to do.

S.G.

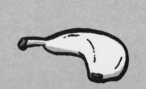

When you discover a gorilla in your bathtub, you've first got to decide whether or not it's okay for him to stay there.

If you're sure your dad will say "NO",
then you simply must find a way
to get the gorilla out —
        without hurting his feelings —

which would surprise your mother very much!

My, my, but you do have a problem — a BIG problem! And that is exactly why I wrote this book. You see, I have discovered a gorilla in my bathtub on several occasions, so I have a pretty good idea on how to get one out.

No, no, no — laying a trail of bananas
to the door won't work!
Gorillas like bathtubs better.

And please don't try putting a rope around its tummy.
Gorillas do not like ropes around their tummies.

It reminds them of being tangled in a bowl of spaghetti.

Come now, I can assure you that bringing another gorilla over to play in the backyard is a waste of time.

If your gorilla wanted to play with another gorilla, he wouldn't have come to visit YOU in the first place!

Oh dear, dear...
I can see you are going to need a lot of help.

Since you're so smart, you might think of turning on the water to frighten the gorilla — but don't! What if the gorilla brought his swimming suit?

Now you could order another bathtub and have it delivered to the front yard and hope the gorilla will switch,

but how will you explain that to the neighbors?

What about taking a two-week trip to your grandmother's house, you ask? Maybe the gorilla will get lonely and go home.

Good idea — but then he might just follow you and get into your grandmother's bathtub instead.

Besides, he knew his mother was at the hair salon anyway.

My dear friend, please, please try not to be frustrated.

If the gorilla is still in your bathtub, I should like to tell you that the very best way to get him out is simply to say,

Because gorillas are really very friendly and quite easy to get along with —

if you just know how to ask properly.

Well the Gorilla has gone home, and everyone is happy. See how smart you are now? PLEASE is a very special word — isn't it?

Let's practice saying PLEASE so you will never, ever forget it. Just read along with me...

"PLEASE, hand me the towel. That gorilla dripped all over the place!"

"May I play with the rubber ducky, PLEASE?"

"Will you PLEASE not sit on the bananas?"

"Will you PLEASE say 'PLEASE' all the time now?"

"Is it okay if I stop practicing now, PLEASE? I've got it!"

Want to have some more fun? Walk around your house saying 'PLEASE' over and over again just as fast as you can.

"PLEASE PLEASE PLEASE PLEASE PLEASE PLEASE PLEASE PLEASE PLEASE...."